HWS Publishing

ISBN 978-0-9815285-0-2
ISBN 0-9815285-0-3

This book is dedicated
to the many travelers who
make the long trip
and to their families and
friends who support
them while traveling.

Lewis the Duck went into work. He was excited.

His boss, Mr. Wood, had asked to meet with him. Lewis wondered

what he could want.

"Lewis," Mr. Wood said. "You've worked hard for us since the day I took you under my wing. It's time you flew solo on a big project down south. Do a good job and it could mean a big promotion and raise for you!"

That night, Lewis was so excited. He told his wife and kids all about the trip. "This is my big break!" he said. But suddenly he felt sad about leaving his family. "Mr. Wood says I'll be gone for a whole month."

His wife smiled. "It's okay," she said. "Birds of a feather flock together. I'll make sure we keep in touch every day. I'm so proud of you, Lewis!"

The next morning Lewis packed his things, waved goodbye to his wife and kids, and hit the skies. He had no idea what was in store for him!

Lewis flew all day and into the night until he found the city where he would be working. Lewis was tired. He looked for the duck-friendly place to stay that Mr. Wood told him about. When he saw a hotel sign with a picture of a duck, he knew he had found the right place!

THE COFFEE HOUSE

It was Homewood Suites by Hilton®, a hotel just for guests like Lewis who stay for long periods of time. "Good evening, Lewis," said a woman behind the front desk. Her name was Maria, and she said she'd been expecting Lewis.

Maria was so nice! She told Lewis all about his room, the fitness center and how to use the high-speed internet access. They even had a pool. "Make yourself at home," Maria said. Lewis thanked her and went to his suite.

Lewis felt right at home. There was plenty of room to spread his wings. His suite had a kitchen, living room, bedroom, bathroom and dressing area. It was the nicest, most comfortable place he had ever stayed.

L ewis unpacked, soaked in the tub (of course) and called his wife to tell her he had landed safe and sound at Homewood Suites. "I'm so glad, sweetie," his wife said. "Sweet dreams." Then Lewis climbed into bed. And what a bed it was… big, comfy and topped with a pillow that looked custom-made for Lewis.

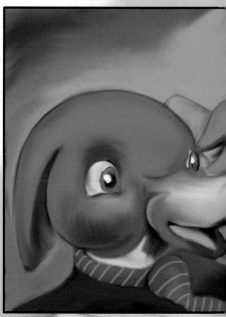

The next morning, Lewis woke up early for work and went to the breakfast buffet. He couldn't believe how much food there was! Frank, the breakfast host, helped Lewis with his plate. When Lewis tried to pay for the meal, Frank just smiled. "Keep your money, Lewis! It's all complimentary." Lewis thanked him and thought, "Wow, everyone is so nice here at Homewood Suites."

That day, Lewis had a great time working on his special project. When he came back to Homewood at the end of the day, he worked out in the fitness center and had a swim before dinner.

At the evening manager's reception, Lewis fixed a plate of lasagna, salad and breadsticks. It was delicious! Ms. Smith, the General Manager, was there helping out. She told Lewis how delighted she was that he was staying for the month. "If you ever need anything just let me know," she said. "And please call me Jan."

W

hen he got back to his suite, he called his wife.

"Honey, you've got to see this place – you would just love it here!"

His wife replied, "I'm glad your trip is going well! Lewis, the kids are so excited. They sent you an email. See if you can open it."

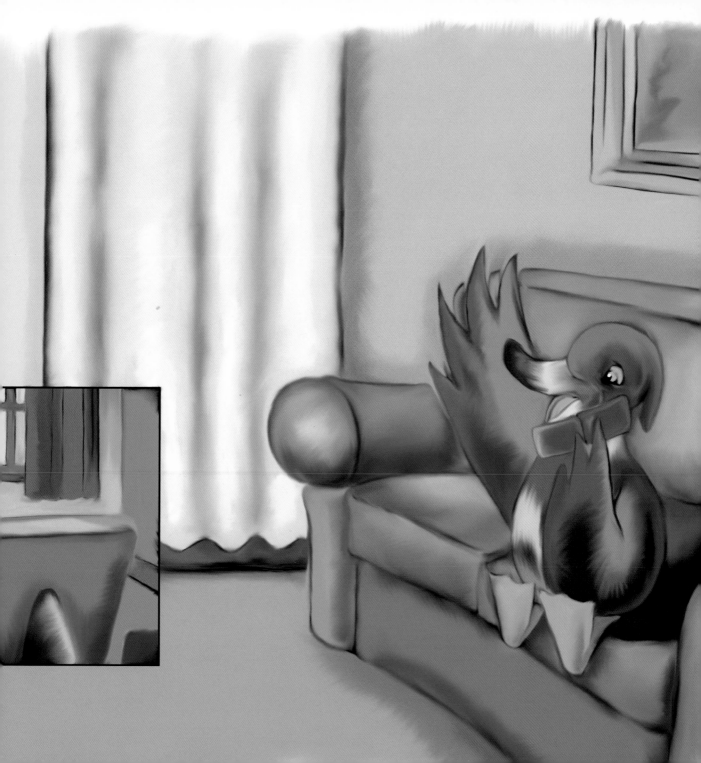

L ewis connected to the internet right away.

Sure enough, there was an email with a video from his kids.

What a surprise! He called to let them know he got it.

He told them he loved and missed them – but the

video made him feel like he was back home.

The days and weeks flew by and before he knew it, Lewis was done with his special job. On the last day, he saw someone familiar in the lodge. It was Mr. Wood! "Lewis, you've done such great work here. I have a new job and a big office waiting for you back home. Why don't you take a couple days off and celebrate with your family? You've earned it."

When Lewis landed on his front step, his family was waiting with open wings. He told them all about the great news from Mr. Wood. And when it came time to celebrate, Lewis took the whole family to the best place he could imagine – to meet his new friends at Homewood Suites.

Author Bio:
Bill Duncan is a duck admirer who lives in Memphis, Tennessee, with his wife Julie and son Christian. This is his first book.

Artist Bio:
Greg Cravens is the creator of the syndicated cartoon, *The Buckets*. He enjoys spending time with his wife Paula and sons Gideon and Cory.

The Story of Lewis

Our guests often ask, "Why the duck?
Who is he and what does a duck have to do with Homewood Suites?"

Homewood Suites chose a duck because it symbolizes versatility and adaptability. Ducks are comfortable in air, in water, and on land. They migrate long distances over extended periods. And their ability to adapt and thrive in a variety of places represents our goal in the travel and hospitality industry – to serve guests with resourcefulness and flexibility.

We chose a wood duck, considered one of the most beautiful creatures in nature. And we've given him a name – Lewis. By naming Lewis and bringing him to life, we've created a visual representation of a unique brand that caters to those who want the comforts of home when on the road for a few days or more. And, with Lewis to guide us, there is no doubt that we will meet our guests' individual needs for comfort, flexibility and convenience.

HOMEWOOD
SUITES
—— Hilton ——